F/JR
GEI

R: 3.2
(K-3)

DATE DUE

12-14-95 (3B)			
2-22-96			

HIGHSMITH 45-220

Pa's Balloon
and Other
Pig Tales

Arthur Geisert

Houghton Mifflin Company

Boston 1984

To my wife, Bonnie

Library of Congress Cataloging in Publication Data

Geisert, Arthur.
    Pa's balloon and other pig tales.

    Summary: A pig family take their new balloon for a
ride, race it, and eventually fly it over the North Pole.
    [1. Pigs – Fiction. 2. Balloon ascensions – Fiction]
I. Title.
PZ7.G2724Pas   1984   [Fic]   83-18552
ISBN 0-395-35381-5

Printed in the United States of America

P   10   9   8   7   6   5   4   3   2   1

Contents

Pa's Balloon
1

One fine afternoon the package truck arrived.
It delivered Pa's kit.

That very night we put it together.

The next morning Ma packed a picnic lunch of all our favorite foods.

Pa inflated the balloon. He told us to speed it up.

Once we were in we all held on tight. Pa cut the
last rope.

Then we were off.

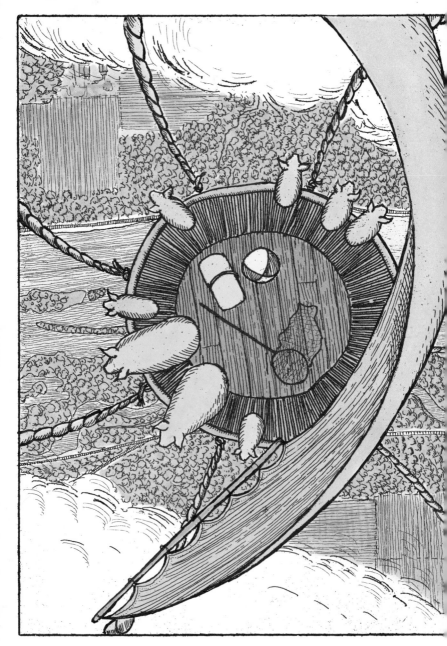

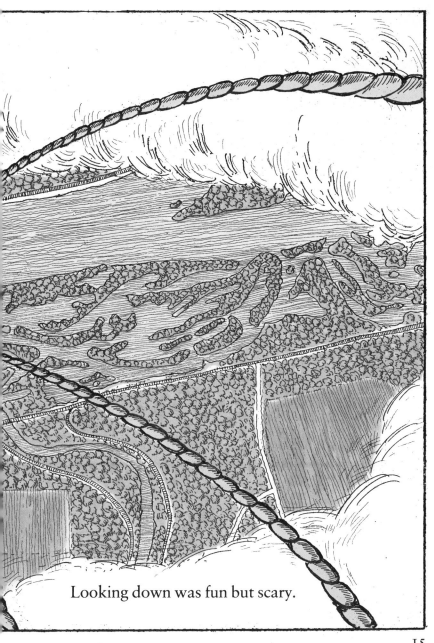

Looking down was fun but scary.

We flew for hours until Pa saw a likely landing place.

We tied the balloon down and unloaded.

Ma took us swimming,

while Pa looked at the view.

After swimming we were all hungry. We had roast corn, potato chips, olives, pickles, orange pop, blueberry pie, and apples. Was it good!

After lunch Ma and Pa took a nap while we played ball. They told us to stay close.

It's a good thing Ma and Pa were asleep.

Then we played hide-and-seek.

I picked a good spot.

It started raining real hard.

25

Ma and Pa loaded up in a hurry . . .

. . . and took off.

Ma and Pa counted the young ones; one was missing!

They quickly turned around and hurried back to the rock. I was waiting and I was scared.

Pa lowered the balloon
and held out the rescue
net. I sure was glad. Ma
and Pa were relieved.

Then we were off for home.

We made it by sundown. Ma took us inside,
fed us, and put us to bed.
Pa put the balloon away.

33

The day was clear and mild.
Everyone was here for the big race.

Pa was ready!

We were waiting
for the starting
cannon.

39

Pa was the first to set his sail.

The others were slower.

By the time the others got their sails set we were far ahead.

That put us in first place.

The last-place balloon was jealous.

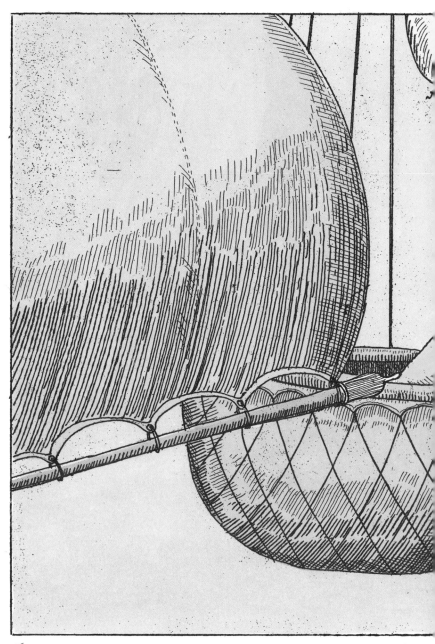

They decided to cheat.

ST. GEORGE SCHOOL,
LINN, MISSOURI

47

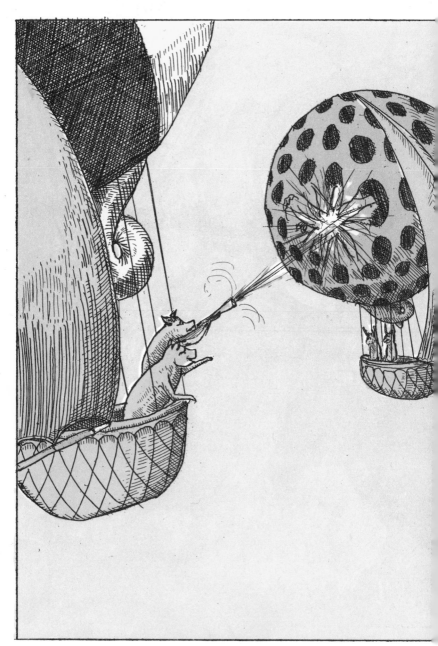

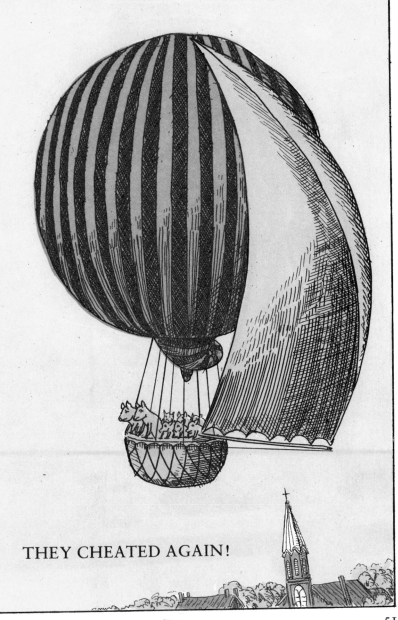

THEY CHEATED AGAIN!

Ma and Pa watched helplessly.
They knew we were next.

But I had an idea.

The cheaters got close.

Pa was mad and yelled, "YOU PIGHEADS!"

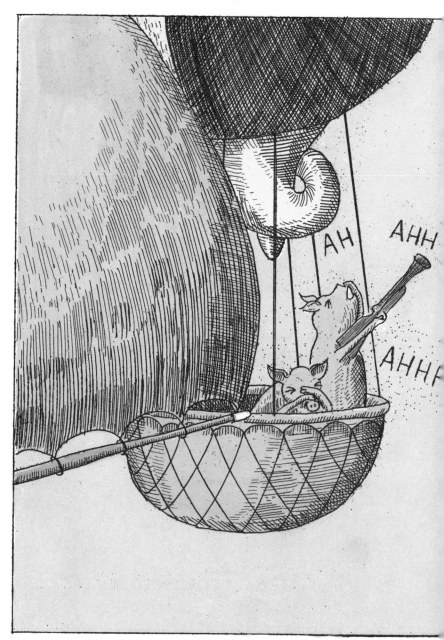

AH AHH

AHHH

Before they pulled the trigger, I threw pepper
at them.

They shot themselves down.

I was surprised how well my idea worked.

Ours was the only balloon to finish.

They gave the prize to me.

The cheaters were put in jail.

They had to patch all the balloons they shot down.

Over the North Pole
3

Pa thought it would be fun to be the first to fly
over the North Pole in a balloon. Ma didn't like
the idea but finally agreed. We were all ready to
go, but we couldn't go right away because it would
take a lot of preparation.

The first thing Pa got was a stove to keep
the air inside the balloon warm in such a cold
place. The package truck delivered it.

Pa had us fill sandbags with coal for the stove. We gathered wood, too. Oak and hickory. Ma kept busy in the house.

The night before we left Ma washed our scarves.
Pa studied his maps and checked his navigation
instruments. Ma packed food that wouldn't spoil —
peanut butter sandwiches and raisins.

The next morning we loaded up.

Pa stoked up the stove. It took a long time to fill the balloon. Then it didn't budge.

Our load was too heavy. It took a lot more stoking
to get us off the ground.

But finally we were off. Pa set the course: due north.
We flew all day and into the night.

The northern lights were beautiful that first night.
And it was so quiet.

The next morning we woke up in a dark cloud.

It was a swarm of mosquitoes. Pa took the balloon
higher, but it was too late. We itched all day.
We scratched and scratched and scratched.

Later that day the balloon dropped, and a polar bear took a swipe at us.

But all he got was a sack of coal and a few icicles.

Then we stopped on top
of an iceberg to get fresh
water.

My stupid brother slipped on the ice and fell in.

Ma tried to dry his scarf,
but it froze stiff as a board.

Pa took a sighting.
He said we were very close
to the North Pole.

We flew a short distance. Pa said, "This is it.
We are over the North Pole!"
"There isn't anything here!" Ma said. "Just ice,
cold, and snow. Let's go home."

Pa said, "We can only go south from here."

We were cold, tired, and hungry.
Then we ate dinner. The raisins were
frozen and felt like little rocks in our
mouths.

The sun was a welcome sight the next morning.
My brother's scarf thawed.

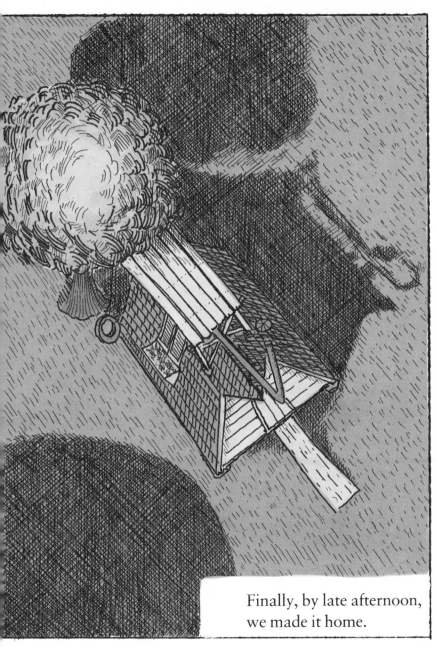

Finally, by late afternoon,
we made it home.

Pa said, "Well, we did it."

"Yes, we sure did," Ma answered. Ma fixed us hot soup and put us to bed. Bed was warm and felt good.

We went to sleep.